For Peter
with love and thanks

Clarion Books
a Houghton Mifflin Company imprint
215 Park Avenue South, New York, NY 10003
Text and Illustrations copyright © 1992 by Cathryn Falwell
Printed in Singapore

Library of Congress Cataloging-in-Publication Data
Falwell, Cathryn.
Nicky loves Daddy / Cathryn Falwell.
p.   cm.
Summary: Nicky experiences new sensations through his five senses
when his loving father takes him out in his stroller.
ISBN 0-395-60820-1
[1. Senses and sensation—Fiction.   2. Babies—Fiction.
3. Fathers and sons—Fiction.]   I. Title.
PZ7.F198Nim   1992
[E]—dc20   90-21494
CIP
AC

TWP   10   9   8   7   6   5   4   3   2   1

Nicky Loves Daddy

Cathryn Falwell

CLARION BOOKS
NEW YORK

Eyes to see.
What does
Nicky see?

Daddy —
ready for
a walk.

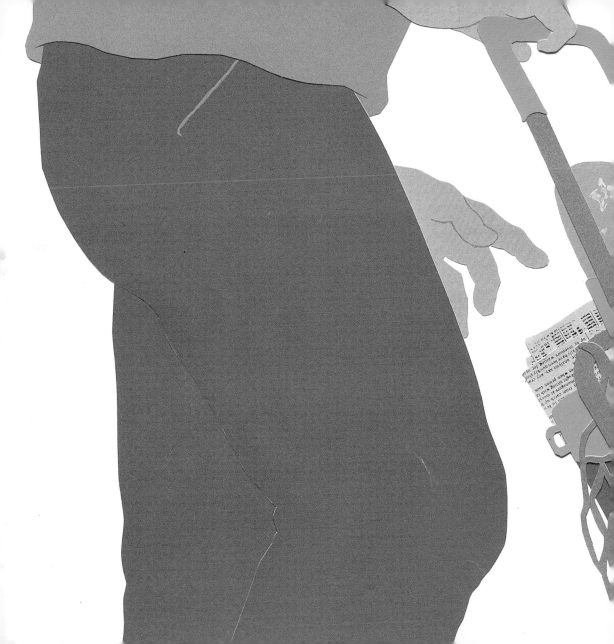

Ears to hear.
What does
Nicky hear?

Woof, woof! Beep, beep!

A dog going
for a ride.

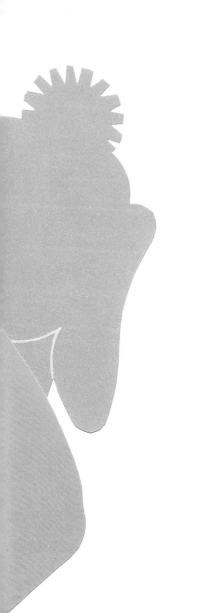

A nose to smell.

What does
Nicky smell?

Mmmm!
Donuts!

Hands to touch.
What does
Nicky touch?

A soft
bunny
and a
sticky
donut.

A mouth
to taste.

What does
Nicky taste?

Cold milk
and a
sweet treat.

Yum!

A heart to love.

Who does
Nicky love?

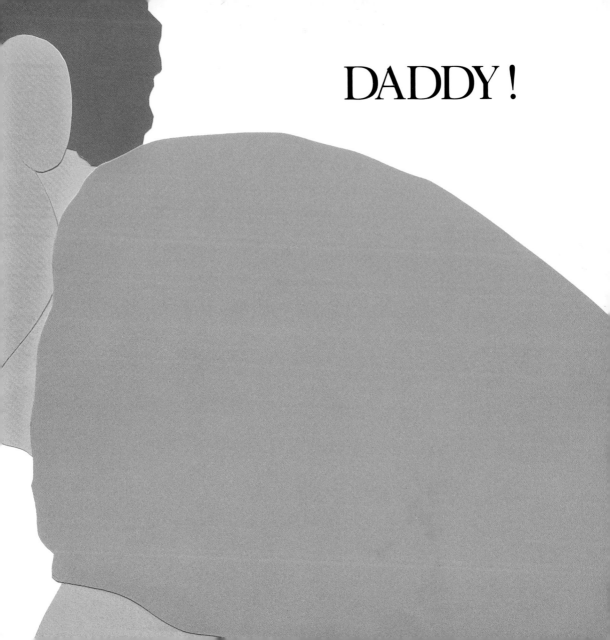

DADDY !